The Su

Teaching Notes

This book contains the following vowels:
a e i o u.

This book contains the following consonants:
b c d d f g h j m n s t w

This book contains the following non-phonetic sight words:
a from I the under was we were

Prior to Reading:

Look at the cover picture with your child. Ask, "What do you think this book might be about?" or "What do you do when the sun is hot?"

While Reading:

Encourage your child to use finger-point reading to track the words across the page. Give them time to decode the word. Avoid jumping in to help too early. If your child gets stuck on a word, prompt them to look at the initial sound of the word and to use the picture for clues. Then sound out the letters with them, scaffolding them to run the sounds together.

After Reading:

Talk about the story. Link the book with their prior knowledge. What things did the people in the story do to keep cool? What did the dog and cat do? Did those things work? Revisit their prediction about what the book was about. Was their prediction correct? Ask what worked in the end to keep everyone cool.

The sun was hot

I was hot. Dad was hot.
Mom was hot.

The dog and cat were hot.

I got a hat. Dad got a hat.
Mom got a hat.

The dog and cat hid from
the sun in the hut.

I was hot. Dad was hot.
Mom was hot.

The dog and cat were hot.

Mom got a jug. Dad got a cup. I got a cup.

The dog and cat hid from the sun in the den.

I was hot. Dad was hot.
Mom was hot.

The dog and cat were hot.

I got a fan. Dad got a fan.
Mom got a fan.

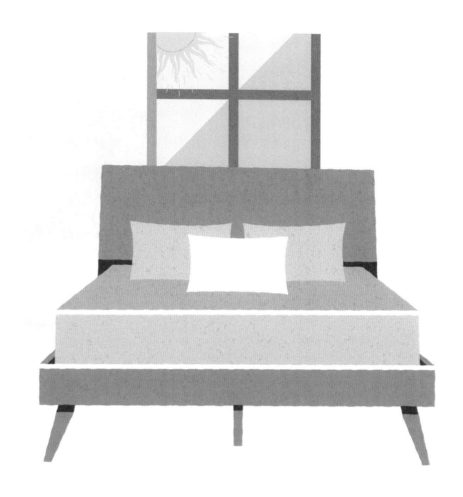

The dog and cat hid from
the sun under the bed.

I was hot. Dad was hot.
Mom was hot.

The dog and cat were hot.

I got wet. Dad got wet.
Mom got wet.

The dog and cat got wet.
We were not hot.

The end.

About this book

This book is part of a series of five phonemic early readers. This pink series goes with the pink language materials in a Montessori classroom. The other books in this series will provide reading experiences with more CVC words, short vowel sounds, consonants and sight words.

Other titles in this series are:
- The Rat Ran.
- Can Pig Nap?
- Bad Dog
- Sam and Pam

Once your child has mastered the pink materials and readers, introduce them to the blue language materials and the five blue phonemic early readers. These will provide reading experiences with longer phonemic words using the same vowel sounds and consonants.

The green series of phonemic readers will provide reading experiences with phonograms, blends and digraphs. They are designed to be introduced when your child has learned the relevant phonograms by using the green language materials.

From the Author

y name is Cath King. I'm a Montessori
acher in New Zealand. I hope you
njoyed this Pink Reader, and that it has
lped you practice reading CVC words. If
u enjoyed this book, please leave a
view on Amazon. I read every review and
ey help new readers discover my books.

et your free printable download of the Pink Reader Word Searches
ps://edu-king.weebly.com/download-pink-reader-word-search.html

Made in the USA
Las Vegas, NV
13 November 2023